WOOD GREEN
ANIMAL SHELTER

Hello. My name is Patricia Casey.

This building is Wood Green Animal

Shelter. It's a place in the city

where sick, stray,

or abandoned

animals are taken care

of. It's always busy.

Happy, sad, and funny things happen

every minute. After visiting a few times,

I decided to bring my camera and

pencils along. I had a plan—to make

you this book!

For Les Rollings—

who told me, "It's the way you touch an animal
for the first time that will gain its confidence"

And for all the staff at
Wood Green Animal Shelter—

thank you for opening your door so many times to share
your experiences with me

A percentage of the royalties from this book is
being donated to Wood Green Animal Shelters,
Registered Charity No. 298348.

The publisher and artist are grateful to
Wood Green Animal Shelters for permission
to make reference to Wood Green Animal Shelter
in the title and content of this book.

First U.S. editon 2001

Library of Congress Cataloging-in-Publication Data is available.
Library of Congress Catalog Card Number 00-047404

ISBN 0-7636-1210-3

10 9 8 7 6 5 4 3 2 1

Printed in Hong Kong

This book was typeset in Futura Bold and Providence Sans.
The illustrations were done in photographic collage,
watercolor, and pencil.

Candlewick Press
2067 Massachusetts Avenue
Cambridge, Massachusetts 02140

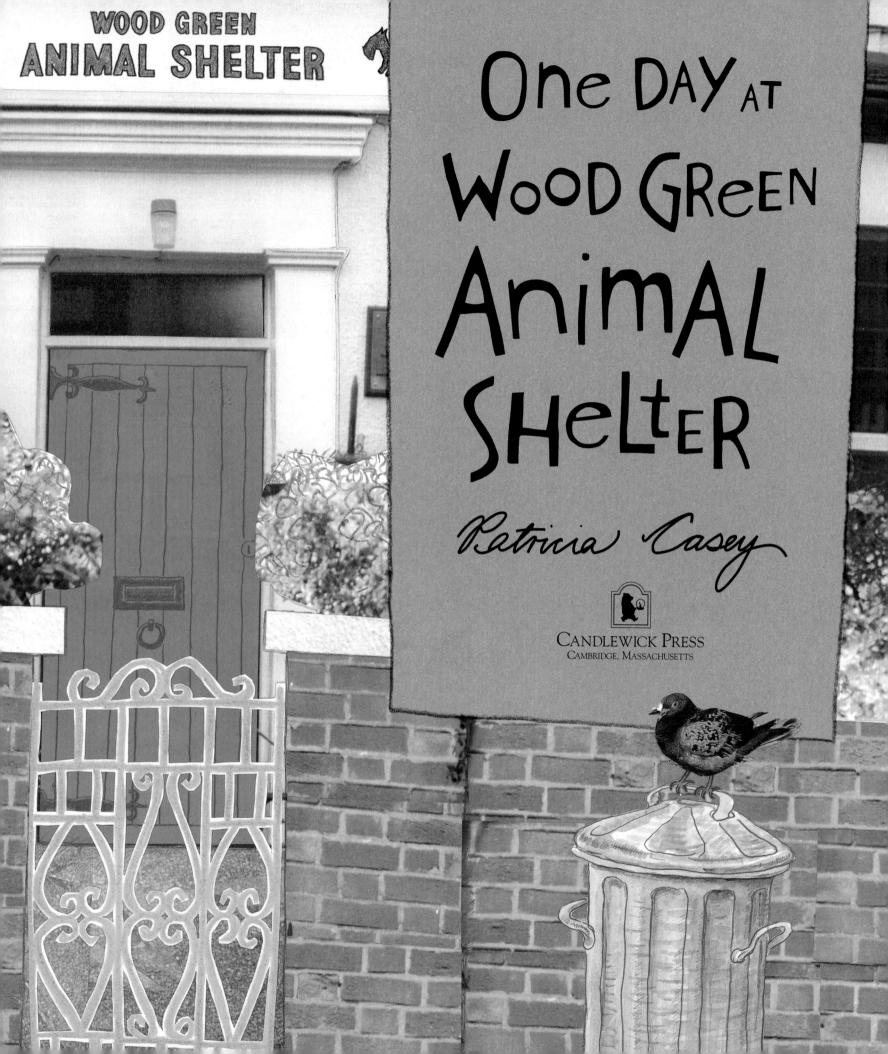

WOOD GREEN
ANIMAL SHELTER

One Day at Wood Green Animal Shelter

Patricia Casey

CANDLEWICK PRESS
CAMBRIDGE, MASSACHUSETTS

The shelter opens at a quarter to eight.
Here comes everyone for work.

Les, the manager, has the keys.
(That's Tandy, his Alsatian dog, on the leash.)
Kelly is carrying a box. (I wonder what's inside?)
Wendy is carrying William, a fox she takes care of.
Debbie, the nurse, has brought Roosevelt, her bulldog.

And I am here too, with my camera.
Penny, the Shelter Cat, is very pleased to see us.
There she is on the doorstep.

"Swee!" cheeps Kelly's box as we go inside. Tandy pads upstairs to Les's office.

CLINIC →

8

Now Angela, Colin, Neil, Rikky, and Alison arrive. Altogether nine people work at the shelter.

Angela gets the waiting room and clinic ready for the day.

Wendy and William go to the downstairs office.

swee

Debbie takes Roosevelt to the back room. Kelly and her cheeping box go too. Alison checks Topsy and Timmy, two stray kittens who stayed overnight.

In the pantry, Colin and Rikky get food ready for the cats who live in the cat sanctuary outside.

Can you hear the cats?
Let's go and see what they are doing.

Look! They're **s t r e t c h i n g**

and **y a w n** ing and **scratching** and **washing**.
They're **uncurling** and **stepping** out of their
little houses. They're **pacing** and
waiting and **thinking** about . . .

Back inside I see what's in Kelly's box. "He's a baby pigeon," Kelly tells me. "He fell out of his nest onto the street. I call him Roast Potato—because he's small enough to fit in my hand, like a potato!"

Roast Potato has a big song for such a small bird!

ROSIE

TOOTS

ARTHUR

Until Roast Potato is old enough to look after himself, Kelly will care for him night and day. Roast Potato is too young to fly, but he likes going for walks.

Swee, swee!

He has a little drink with Timmy the kitten. (They don't know cats and birds don't get along.)

Swee, swee!

He goes for a walk on his pigeon mix.

Sweeeeeee!

He goes for a walk up Roosevelt's back.

It's true!

Roosevelt looks fierce, but he's a softy.
He came to the shelter when he was a
puppy. His owners had been cruel to him.

Debbie took one look at him,
and that was it—**LOVE!**
    She adopted him.
        They go everywhere together.

    Roosevelt's tail is so short that when
he's happy he wags his whole bottom.

    His skin looks too big for him.
        He is all crinkles and wrinkles
        and creases and folds.

· ROSIE ·   · TOOTS ·   · FLUFF ·   · SNAZZLE ·   · SP

Cat Quench

The smoothest part of Roosevelt is his big pink tongue. It is always out instead of in! He gives the kittens' tummies a good lick—just as if he were their mommy. Then he gives Roast Potato's tummy such a good lick, Roast Potato falls over.

It's true!

William, the fox, came to the shelter with his sister, Anna, when they were only three days old.

"They were unearthed from their burrow under a building site," says Wendy. "Anna was a healthy cub. But William was sick. First he had colic, then pneumonia, and next he went bald!"

While we talk, William lets me stroke him. Now his fur is thick and silky soft. His eyes are red-gold. They can see in the dark.

I ask where Anna is.
"She was released back into the wild,"
Wendy tells me. "But William was ill
for months. To nurse him properly,
we had to hold and touch him. So he
grew used to people. He couldn't
survive in the wild now."

William yawns. It's his bedtime.
(Foxes sleep in the day, not the night.)
Wendy lays him in his straw outside.

**"Good morning, William.
Sleep tight," I say.**

Twelve o'clock is clinic time. Dr. Simmonds, the vet, is ready to see his first patient, Rolley. The waiting room is full of pets and people. Everyone is chatting. Colin takes notes.

LIQUID PARAFFIN

ALCOHOL

cotton

tweezers

scissors

waste bowl

VITAMIN SOLUTION

Dr. Simmonds listens to Rolley's heart through his stethoscope.
Boom, boom, boom. "That sounds like a steady beat," he says.

bandage

Shampoo
Wet coat and
leave for 2 mins
Rinse
Repeat weekly

clippers

Ear
Drops

thermometers

SKIN
SCRUB

FLEA
AWAY
POWDER

Carlos knows that Rolley is never scared with Dr. Simmonds.
Debbie gets more heart pills. "One a day, with food," she says.

I go upstairs to visit Les, the manager, and Tandy. "Someone just called to say she saw a young deer in the cemetery," Les says. "It needs to be with other deer. Will you and Neil go and rescue it in the ambulance?"

ZOOM BrooM!

Neil and I find the deer asleep behind a gravestone!

We are just about to catch it with our blanket when . . .

HUP!

It leads Neil on a real wild-deer chase!

Don't be frightened, deery.

We drive the frightened little deer to a wood where Neil knows other deer live. I open the back door and . . .

HUP!

Back at the shelter, lots of new animals have arrived.

Angela is feeding a baby hedgehog with warm goat's milk. "A little boy found it in his garden. It was all alone without a mother," she tells us.

She shows me a dazed song thrush. "It bumped into a lady's greenhouse," she tells me. "Soon it will be well enough to fly away."

Rikky is dusting a cat with flea powder. "She's a 'doorstep cat,'" he says. "Someone didn't want her, so they rang the bell and ran away. It happens a lot."

Debbie and Kelly are bandaging splints around a pigeon's broken leg. "Pigeons' legs are so small," says Debbie, "we use lollipop sticks. It should be healed in two weeks."

Alison tells me about a little girl who brought in a gecko. "It climbed into her mom's suitcase when they were in Spain," she says. "They didn't find it until they unpacked. It's come a long way. They don't know how to take care of it, so we will."

"Another little girl tried to bring her lame pony right into the clinic!" Les tells me. "I told them to wait outside. This is not a stable!"

The day is nearly over. Colin's made some coffee. What a busy day it's been! Everyone deserves a cup.

William has woken up.
He likes coffee for his breakfast too.
Mmmm! Coffee fingers.

William may be wide-awake,
but the other animals are tired.
Sleep well, Timmy and Topsy.

Good night, Doorstep Cat.
Good night, Gecko.
Good night,
Lollipop Pigeon.

The baby hedgehog will need feeding through
the night. Angela makes
a nest to carry it home.

The cats in the cat sanctuary
are curling up.

Roast Potato and Roosevelt
are waiting
to go home.
So is Tandy.

Penny will see
everyone again tomorrow.

Good night, everyone.
Good night,
Wood Green Animal Shelter,
until another day.

Index

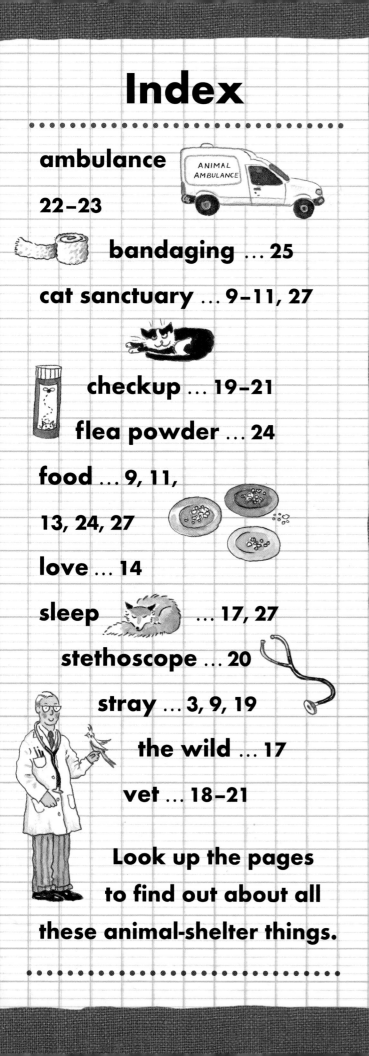
Look up the pages to find out about all these animal-shelter things.

About the Artist

Patricia Casey has written and illustrated several books for children — but this is the first time she has used a camera and a tape recorder to help her.